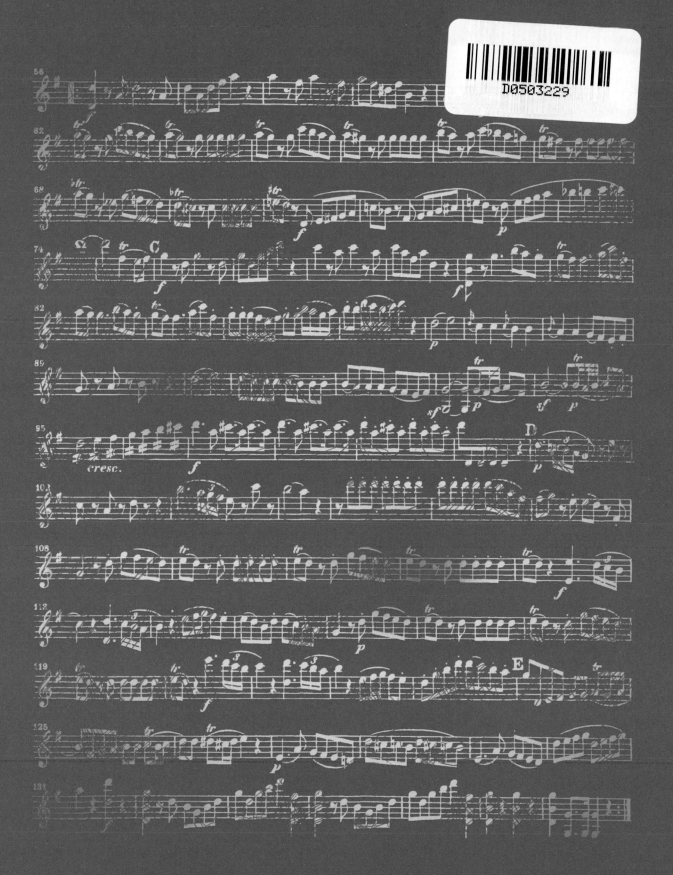

A Violin for Elva

MARY LYN RAY

ILLUSTRATED BY
TRICIA TUSA

HOUGHTON MIFFLIN HARCOURT
Boston   New York

www.hmhco.com

The illustrations in this book were done in watercolor and ink.
The text type was set in Fifteen 36.
The display type was set in Peoni Pro.
Selected music calligraphy by Judythe Sieck

LIBRARY OF CONGRESS CATALOGING-IN-PUBLICATION DATA
Ray, Mary Lyn.
  A violin for Elva / Mary Lyn Ray ; illustrated by Tricia Tusa.
      pages cm
Summary: As a child, Elva asks for a violin so that she can make beautiful
music but many years pass before her dream can come true.
ISBN 978-0-15-225483-4
[1. Violin—Fiction. 2. Determination (Personality trait)—Fiction.]
I. Tusa, Tricia, illustrator. II. Title.
 PZ7.R210154Vio 2014
 [E]—dc23
 2013042839

Manufactured in China
SCP 10 9 8 7 6 5 4 3 2 1
4500499893

For all who hear what Elva heard
—M.L.R.

For Rhe
—T.T.

Above the ruffle of talk
and the rustle of dresses,

Elva heard music.

Later, she didn't say she had been watching through a hedge. All she told her parents was—

"I want a violin."

She asked them both.
She asked with *please*.
But they hadn't heard
what Elva heard.
And they said no.

So she pretended.

When she should have been brushing her teeth,
Elva was rehearsing for recitals.

When she could have been
learning subtraction,

or should have been going to sleep, she
was playing music only she could hear.

Summer, autumn, winter, spring, Elva played.
And Elva grew. She outgrew her sleeves, outgrew her shoes.
She grew until she was a grownup—and outgrew her violin.

Now she had a briefcase and a job.
She had appointments and important meetings.

But if she saw a page tremulous with music,
she remembered what she once had wanted.

"I'm much too busy," Elva said, though she began
to borrow records from the library downtown.
At home, she listened to them.
And then she felt she had picked up her violin again.

Sometimes she was the whole string section
of the philharmonic, all those elbows going
up and down. Other times she played alone.

But the music stopped
when the records stopped—

and silence filled the room.

Elva had a dog for conversation.
But conversation with her dog couldn't cover up the quiet.
She kept chocolates for refreshment.
But chocolates couldn't fill the empty feeling.

"Well, I have things to do," said Elva.
And she did them.

So summer, autumn, winter, spring, the years went by.
Elva had many satisfactions and achievements.
Only one was missing.
"I'm too old now," she told her dog.

But more and more she kept imagining
what might have been—

until one day she took a breath

and took her purse,
    and bought a shiny,
        fragile, varnished . . .

VIOLIN.

At home Elva studied how to hold it.
Then she lifted it against her shoulder
and clamped it with her chin.
She pushed the bow across a string.

SQUEEEK.
She tried again.
SQUEEEEEEEEEEEK.

So Elva tried something else.
She drew the bow back toward her—and the string sang.
A single note was not exactly music.
But it gave her expectations.

Feeling bold, she tried a different string.
The bow bucked. The dog slid under the sofa.
But Elva played her one note again and was encouraged.
"I will improve," she said.

But she didn't.

It wasn't easy: holding the bow correctly,
landing on the right notes,
figuring out flats and sharps.
"I will improve," she said.

But still she didn't.

So Elva sadly snapped the case
and put away her violin.

Then one day she heard that
Madame Josephina was
accepting beginning students.

And again she took a breath and took her purse—
and bought a course of lessons.

Every Tuesday, every Thursday,
Elva came to Madame Josephina.

On the days between, she practiced.

Then there was a recital. All the students had to perform onstage. Everyone was nervous. Especially Elva. But she drew the bow against the strings—and in that moment something happened.

Elva was making music.

She came right home—
and, lifting her violin, she played for her dog.
Then she played again for herself.
And again. And again. And again—

until, at last, Elva kissed her bow
and went to bed,
imagining all the tomorrows.
And all the music there was to make.